This book belongs to:

_____

Published by Small World, Big Imaginations Ltd www.smlworld.co.uk
Copyright © Irvine Gersch, Bertie Caplan, Jessica Caplan, 2021

ISBN 9781910966525

Printed and bound in Great Britain.

OF THE LITTLE

Do you know why we all need our sleep?

Have you ever noticed how when you wake up you feel good?

And if you didn't feel too well, or are worried before you went to sleep,

you often wake up feeling much better the next day?

So, what could possibly be happening?

Well here's one idea that might explain it.

During the night, when you are fast asleep, little tiny sleep doctors come to visit you, and work really hard to make you feel good, to feel well and to feel happy. They want you to feel great the next day.

Their names are Lilly and Billy, Zac and Jack, Hettie and Lettie. They also have a helper called Lionel. Each tiny sleep doctor has a tiny, tiny white suit, and a little white helmet, and each of them has a special set of tools. Lionel has a blue helmet and blue dungarees.

This is what happens –
When you are asleep the little team of sleep doctors get ready to visit you. They love to help.

Their hospital, which is so small that we can't even see it, is based in the middle of your brain. Before they leave their hospital, they check what they need to do to help.

They are so, so, so small that they can easily stand on the top of a pin.
Yes, that small.

3

This is a story about a time when they visited Amy.

Amy was 6 years old. She was a very good girl, who was kind and worked hard at school. She loved playing with her friends, singing and dancing.

On special days her parents took her out to see horses, which she loved.
Amy could be a little clumsy, and sometimes she did not look where she was going.

Sometimes Amy worried about things. For example, sometimes she worried about getting an answer wrong in class, in front of the other children, and thought that the children might laugh at her. She also worried about her wobbly tooth falling out, and a new one not growing back. She worried when she had a tummy ache, in case it wouldn't get better soon.

So, one night, Amy told her mummy she had a little pain on her gum above her front tooth. She had also fallen over and hurt her finger that same day.

She was very worried that her finger would not get better, and she wouldn't be able to do her drawings and writing at school.
"Don't worry," said her mummy – "you go to sleep. Leave it to me. I have an idea."

That night, her mummy phoned the sleep doctors to help.

But remember, they are very, very, very tiny.
They are so small that they can stand on the top
of a pin.

And when they do things it takes them much,
much longer than us.

Lionel answered the phone and heard all
about Amy, and then told the others.
The sleep doctors, Lilly and Billy, Zac and Jack,
Lettie and Hettie, and of course, Lionel, the
helper, all put on their special uniforms and got
ready.

They got ready quickly.
Well, when I say "quickly" – for them, it was
quick, but for us we would think it was very
slow.

Lionel took quite a long time to put on his
uniform because he was very slow to dress.
In fact, Lionel got mixed up and put his
dungarees on back to front. The sleep doctors
said, "Oh Lionel – look at your dungarees! "
Lionel looked a bit embarrassed but everyone
was very kind and helped him turn his
dungarees round the right way.

So, it took them an hour to get ready.

7

Then, the sleep doctors got into their tiny, tiny ambulance.

It was Lionel's job to close the back door and to lock it. However, this time, he forgot to lock it. When they started the engine, the door opened. Poor Lionel nearly fell out.
The others had to pull him back in, by his arms. Lionel was very embarrassed.

"Don't worry," said the sleep doctors. "We are just pleased that you haven't hurt yourself."

Now all safely in their tiny ambulance, the little sleep doctors drove all the way to Amy's tongue really quickly.
Well, when I say "quickly," I mean it took them about an hour to travel from their little hospital in their tiny, tiny, tiny ambulance to Amy's tongue.

It was only a small distance for us, but for the tiny sleep doctors, it seemed like a very long way.

8

The team arrived, and popped onto Amy's tongue. Luckily, she had cleaned her teeth well. The sleep doctors loved it, because it smelled all fresh and lovely. Then they looked around for the work that they needed to do.

The leader of the sleep doctors, whose name was Lilly, told the team to look for the sore gum and prepare their ladders to climb up.

The team carried a little ladder and a slide. They used them to go up and down and around easily.

The team divided up into pairs or twos. Each pair had a special job to do.

The first pair, Lilly and Billy, had the job of hoovering away all the red sore dots on the gum. They were the Hoover team.

They had a tiny, tiny soft hoover.

11

Then came the second team, Zac and Jack.
Their job was to use a dustpan and brush to
clear up any red dots that had fallen down.
They were the Sweeper team.

This team cleaned all around until everything
was really nice and clean.

And finally, the last team, Lettie and Hettie –
the Polishers. They cleaned the whole area with
a tiny, tiny, tiny spot of polish until it all looked
smooth, clean and beautiful.

Each pair did their special job really well.

Lionel watched everyone do their job. He
stood nearby in case anyone needed his help.

What a good job they had done!
After they had finished that job, they got ready
for their second job in Amy's finger.

She had scraped it that same day at school
when she fell over. It happened because she
wasn't looking carefully where she was going.

Well, for the tiny, tiny sleep doctors it was a long, long way down from Amy's gum to her finger.

They would have to go across to Amy's shoulder, down her arm, and all the way to her hand, and then to her middle finger.

For us, that is a very small distance, but for the tiny sleep doctors, it is a very long way.
Lionel came with the little sleep doctors as well. He was ready to help.

They set up their slide and got ready to slide all the way down to Amy's hand.

They really rushed to get there, and went as fast as they could.

But remember, although it would only take us a few seconds to go that far, it was so far for the little sleep doctors that it took them more than an hour to get there.

And then poor Lionel, who was not sitting up properly, got stuck at the end of the slide.
The others had to pull him out.

Anyway, when they all finally got to the middle finger, they found a few little bits of red dots inside.

15

The three teams got ready for their special jobs.

First, Lilly and Billy, the Hoover team, cleared the few tiny red hurty bits which they found.

Then, the second team, the Sweeper team, Zac and Jack, did the same with a dustpan and brush.

And finally, the Polisher Team, Lettie and Hettie, got their tiny, tiny, tiny spot of polish ready. They cleaned the whole finger, to clear away all the hurty bits.

Then, Lionel shone his tiny torch to check that everything was ok, and was very pleased to shout, "All done!," in a loud, important voice. The sleep doctors thanked Lionel for telling them, but asked him to whisper, in case he woke Amy up.

Now they had to get back to the ambulance. They did this by climbing a special ladder which they had with them.

They rushed up the ladder as fast as they could.

Well, when I say "fast, " it actually took them more than two hours.

They arrived safely back to Amy's tongue and jumped back into their ambulance.

Lionel jumped a bit too hard, and bounced up and down five times on Amy's tongue before he could get back in the ambulance.

16

But before they got back to their hospital, there was one last stop they had to make. This was to the "worry room," - the place where all your worries are kept.

It was Lionel's job to open the worry room door. Then, he would shine his torch and look everywhere very carefully. If he then saw any worries at all, he had a hose with him, which he used in order to wash all the worries away. He loved this job because he could turn the water on and off. Sometimes he turned the hose on for much too long and got himself soaked.

Lionel looked very hard all round the "worry room". He used his torch to help him see everything. He spotted all of Amy's worries. He saw her worries about school, which were all a square shape. He saw her worry about the wobbly tooth, which was a long sausage shape, and he saw her worry about her finger which was a roundy shape. Looking very carefully, he also saw a few more tiny worries in the corner.

Lionel turned on his hose, full power, and washed all these worries clean away. As soon as the water went on them, they totally disappeared. It was like magic. Now, all the worries had been completely washed away. The worry room was empty.

Lionel stood up straight, and using his loud and important voice, shouted, "All done!".

19

The sleep doctors gently reminded him again to speak very softly, so as not to wake Amy up. Lionel said he would really try to remember this, for next time. Luckily, he hadn't woken Amy up at all that night.

When Lionel finished washing away all of Amy's worries, he jumped back into the little ambulance. The sleep doctors and Lionel all drove safely home to their little hospital – where they all lived.

They were so tired after all their work, that they went straight to sleep.

In fact, Lionel fell fast asleep in the ambulance!

What a good job they had all done!
The sleep doctors had worked so hard whilst Amy had been fast asleep.

In the morning, Amy woke up feeling wonderful, happy, strong and with no aches and pains.

Her finger was completely better and her gum felt fine too. All her worries had gone.

Mummy said, "How are you, Amy?"

Amy replied, "I feel really great. I don't know what has happened."

But we do.

We know exactly what happened - don't we?

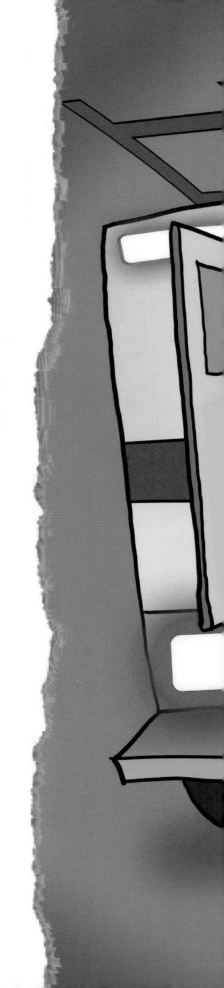

20

Information for Parents/Carers and how to use this book

- This story book was designed to help young children with anxieties and sleep disruptions.

- The story was written by an educational and child psychologist, with more than 40 years' experience of working with many children with such difficulties, and was created together with, and advised by his grandchildren, Jessica (6) and Bertie (10).

- The book was written during the COVID-19 pandemic when so many children experienced anxiety issues, and we hope that this book will be of help to them.

- The story is meant to be used as part of an existing programme to help children with sleep or anxiety difficulties. It is an addition to, not a substitute for, such interventions.

- The story is intended to take the child's mind away from negative thinking and to help them focus on wellness, the positive aspects of our body's strength and resilience, and the importance of sleep.

- The following section will provide a few notes and tips for parents and carers, which hopefully will make this book part of a wider programme.

- It is important to stress that there is no right or wrong way for all children, and we often need to experiment and adapt our programmes to suit. And of course, we always need to find out what works best for each child and family.

- Professional help for children should be sought if problems persist, for example through one's GP or from a specialist clinical or child and educational psychologist.

- We think children will enjoy the idea of sleep doctors. However, in the unlikely event that the idea is experienced as unsettling, parents should explain that this is simply a fictional story. and provide relevant reassurance - using their own form of words.

Some tips and ideas

1.   *Discussing any anxieties – real or imagined.*

Discussion of anxieties is important, and it is vital to hear them out, even if they sound totally unrealistic and "silly" - because they are real and important to your child. They can be discussed in all sorts of ways and reassurance can be provided. However, listening respectfully is a vital first step. Some parents write the worries down and ceremoniously throw them away. One can also discuss how likely it would be for the events which cause anxiety, to actually happen. Remember these are real worries for the child, and thus must be taken seriously, and discussed sensitively and respectfully.

2.   *The bedtime story and the brain*

The story is meant as a disruptor of any negative thoughts, and as a vehicle for putting the child in a good mood for sleep. Of course, any favourite story can be used for this purpose. This story was designed to amuse and please young children, to reassure them and teach them about some of the benefits and importance of sleep. The true brain functions and biochemical healing processes are not dissimilar from the metaphor of sleep doctors. The interested parent may wish to review the biology, neuropsychology, brain science and biochemistry of healing, anxiety and sleep further, and eventually, when the child is ready, to tell them what really happens in greater depth.

3.   *A reward system and Star Chart*

A reward system is a very powerful tool for use with young children. There are many such systems available involving the use of a chart so the child can both see, and be rewarded for, any progress. The system does need to have very clear, specified positive behavioural targets, in words the child can understand. Such targets should state what we want the child to do, rather than what we do not want them to do. And they should be easy to achieve, gradually and slowly building the degree of challenge. For example, depending upon the nature of the problem and what the child can cope with, it might be " to go to sleep by a certain time " or " to stay in bed until 6 am "or" to reduce the number of awakenings to a set number." It should have a clear recording system – with a slow build-up of ticks or stars leading to a reward at the end. The reward should be something that the child really wants. It is sometimes useful for the child to be able to earn mini-rewards along the way. There are many examples of star charts which can be found on-line, but it is always good for a child and parent to create their own. A Chart is best displayed in a place where the child can see it easily and often. Ticks and stars should never be taken away for bad behaviour, as that will weaken the power of the tool. The Chart should last for about 3 or 4 weeks.

4. *A relaxation activity*

Meditation and relaxation provide further powerful tools to help children sleep and manage anxieties. There are many examples provided for adults in this area. For relaxation activities to work for children, these need to be simplified and adapted to the individual child. It would be helpful for parents/carers to listen to some of the many audiotapes or podcasts available, to get an idea of what is needed.

My preferred use with children is in three stages :

(a) getting the child to make each part of their body feel heavy, whilst breathing gently and slowly;

(b) guided imagery of them relaxing on an air bed in a swimming pool, on a warm beautiful day, and then finally;

(c) imagining a return to their own room, feeling warm, safe and comfortable in their own bed.

On each occasion, the child is invited to feel a part of their body as heavy, comfortable and relaxed by the adult specifying this very slowly, with increasingly long spaces between the words. Silence between the words is very important and the procedure should be undertaken very slowly and not rushed.

5.*Self—settling behaviour*

Various sleep programmes recommend interval training e.g. the parents leave the child for longer and longer periods between visits, and/or reduce the time staying next to the child. There are many published books on this subject. What is important is that children do need the opportunity to learn their own series of mini behaviours and rituals to fall asleep. Thus, ideally, they should manage that final stage on their own. These rituals may include several turnings of the pillow, placing their toys in a certain position, having special items with them or lying in the right place. (We adults also have these rituals, by the way.) When children are suffering from separation anxiety we have sometimes introduced a doll or item of clothing scented with the favourite perfume used by the parent, as a reassuring reminder. This could help some children.

The Authors

Emeritus Professor Irvine Gersch
BA (Hons). PGCE. DipEdPsych. PhD. FHEA. FBPsS. PGDipCoaching.
Irvine is a Consultant Educational and Child Psychologist, who has published widely on psychological topics, including listening to children and parenting. He has worked as a teacher, principal educational psychologist of a London Borough, Director of training for educational and child psychologists, government advisor, supervisor, coach and mediator. He is a Fellow of the British Psychological Society and twice winner of the British Psychological Society prize for outstanding contributions to professional psychology. Most importantly, he is Jessica's and Bertie's Papa (Grandfather).

Jessica Caplan (6) is a co-author and Irvine's granddaughter. She loves horses, singing, dancing, playing with her friends, and her two cats.

Bertie Caplan (10) is a co-author, has provided ideas about the illustrations for this book, and is Irvine's grandson. He loves football, drumming, acting, singing and dancing, and Harry Potter.

Acknowledgements

Special thanks go to Barbara Gersch for her invaluable advice about every stage of the development of this book.

We would also like to thank Belinda Ferreira, our Publisher, for her support, encouragement and advice throughout the project.

Printed in Great Britain
by Amazon

22844604R00018